This book belongs to

....

For Victoria and Yvonne

The Pancake Girl: Frankie and Peaches Tales of Total Kindness

Copyright © 2019 by Lisa S. French. All rights reserved. No part of this book may be reprinted or reproduced or utilized in any form or by any electronic, mechanical or other means now known or hereafter invented, including photocopying or recording, or in any information storage or retrieval system, without permission in writing from the publisher.

Favorite World Press LLC, New York, NY
www.favoriteworldpress.com

For information please contact Favorite World Press.
E-mail: hello@favoriteworldpress.com

Text: Lisa S. French
Illustrations: Srimalie Bassani
Interior design: Lisa S. French
Cover design: Lisa S. French and Srimalie Bassani

Library of Congress Control Number: 2018902077

ISBN: 978-1-948751-01-8

In the town of Thanks-Welcome,
up on Can I Help? Hill,
behind a house blue and yellow,
next to a house yellow and blue,
sat an eight-sided house
that wasn't quite pink and wasn't quite red.
Some called the strange color salmon
with a double-whoa shake of the head.

This house was called Tulips.
It was the home of two girls,
one with long, floppy ears
and one with long, floppy curls.

In the tippy-top window
they sat side by side,
elbow to elbow,
watching shooting stars glide.

As they clapped at their friends in the big, Sunday-night sky, Frankie thanked them for coming and sighed a big, Sunday-night sigh.

"Peaches, I have something to tell you,
a bad something I fear."
Then Frankie whispered that something
in her dog's droopy, brown ear.

"Math Monday is coming!
What a sad, creepy day!
They say I must learn it,
but there's no how and no way.

"This day I don't like
seems to come every week.
Peaches, what should I do?
Oh, how I wish you could speak!"

Each tick and each tock of her bumble bee clock
made Frankie shake, and made Frankie shiver,
from her head to her toes
then back up to her liver.

So she stomped and she chomped,
then she flopped on her bed,
and blew one perfect pink bubble,
twice the size of her head.

As she blew, Frankie wondered,
and here's what she thought,
"I will make a to-do list.
Mom likes those a lot!

"Hello, darling Mommy,
here's a list of things I must do.
I must do them on Monday.
Please believe me, it's true!

"Make shoes out of marshmallows.
Build a smile machine.
Paint Peaches' nails purple.
Make sure the moon cheese is green.

"So much better than math!"

"I must ride my bike to the zoo
and set the baby big pandas free.
If they have no special plans,
I will invite them to tea.

"I need to grow butterflies
and let them live in my hair,
then make bubble bath pies
for the Thanks-Welcome Fair.

"So as you can see,
school I simply cannot attend.
I'm too terribly busy.
Just ask Peaches, my friend."

"Frankie, please don't stop at the zoo,
or the Mostly Marshmallows store,
the wind farm, Just Jelly Beans,
or the treehouse next door."

"But what about the pandas?
The butterflies for my hair?
And what about creepy Math Monday?
It's totally sad and so completely not fair!"

Outside the Thanks-Welcome School,
behind the old willow trees,
Frankie spied two holey-toed sneakers
below two small, wobbly knees.

"Well, hello," Frankie said to the girl who stared down at her feet. "I really like those tall sneakers, and your glasses are sweet!

"But I do not like math, and it does not like me. It's a very sad subject. Don't you agree?"

"I think numbers are magic!" said the girl.
"You can put them together and take them apart.
They're more exciting than history
and even more fun than art!

"My name is Ruby.
I started school here this fall.
If it weren't for math class,
I don't think I'd come here at all!"

"If you love numbers," said Frankie,
"why not go inside?
Today is creepy Math Monday,
but you've got no reason to hide."

Ruby said, "There's no way and no how
that I'm going in there!
They make fun of my clothes!
They make fun of my hair!

"Plus, I've got holes in my sneakers.
You can see my little big toes.
They also laugh at the freckles
on the tip of my nose.

"Three mean girls plus two mean boys
equal five days a week I hate school.
And though I kind of like being smart,
they make me feel very uncool.

"Math makes me feel fluffy," said Ruby,
"but meansters make me feel flat.
I guess I'm a pancake girl,
and that is just that!"

Frankie looked at the girl
with a big heart that could see,
and what her heart saw was great sadness
behind that old willow tree.

She said, "All alone on the outside is such a sad place to be. Don't worry about the meansters. You can be friends with me!"

"Hey, Frankie, who's your new pal?" Molly snarled.
"Where did she get that weird hair?
Why does she dress like a farmer
at the Thanks-Welcome Fair?"

"My friend's name is Ruby.
She's as smart as can be!
She's a math-a-magician,
just you wait and see!"

But Ruby stood frozen stiff.
She could not write on the board,
which made Molly giggle quite meanly,
as she put her head down and snored.

"Please don't be frightened," said Frankie.
"I'll stay here by your side
while you add and subtract,
multiply and divide."

$$7a - b(4a - 3b) + 9b^2 + 4a =$$
$$7a - 4ab + 3b^2 + 9b^2 + 4a =$$
$$12b^2 - 4ab + 11a$$

Then Ruby showed her math magic,
and no one bothered to tease.
And her most favorite part,
no more wobbly knees!

As a tornado of chalk dust
whirled through the room,
the two new friends said goodbye
to Math Monday gloom!

"Wow!" Sandy coughed.
"That was perfectly cool!
May I offer a sandwich?
Or walk you home after school?"

"Ruby thinks she's so smart," Molly grumbled,
"but she isn't so great.
What's ten gazillion times six?
What's 500 billion times eight?"

"Molly, when you are mean," Frankie sighed,
"Peaches won't do her tricks.
She won't chase her ball,
and she won't fetch her sticks.

"Because we know how we'd feel if someone teased us like that. Just like a bug on a windshield, our feelings would splat!

"We're going to practice math magic.
Would you like to come to my place?
Have a crust of Sandy's whole wheat
to wipe the chalk off your face."

"Well, I could do it for Peaches," Molly said,
"maybe just this one time.
I do have a question for Ruby.
Do you know what makes numbers prime?"

And so Ruby counted all her new friends, plus each and every cloud in the sky, then she sighed a fluffy, happy to *not* be a pancake girl, sigh.

Things to talk about

1. Why did Ruby want to stay home from school every day?

2. How do you think it made Ruby feel when her classmates made fun of how she looked or the clothes that she wore?

3. What do you think it means that Frankie has a "heart that sees"?

4. What did Ruby mean when she said she felt like a pancake girl?

5. How did it make Ruby feel when Frankie stuck up for her?

6. How did Frankie and Ruby help each other beat the Math Monday blues?

7. Why did Molly stop bullying Ruby when she got to know her better?

8. Why did Ruby feel happy and not flat like a pancake when she was with all of her new friends?

Thank you for helping F&P plant a tree!

Favorite World Press will plant one tree for every print or e-book sold from the series Frankie and Peaches: Tales of Total Kindness.

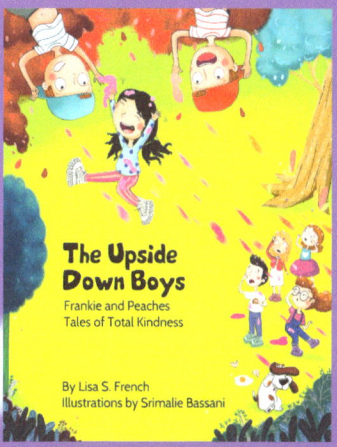
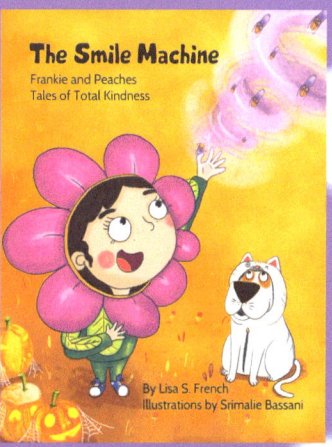

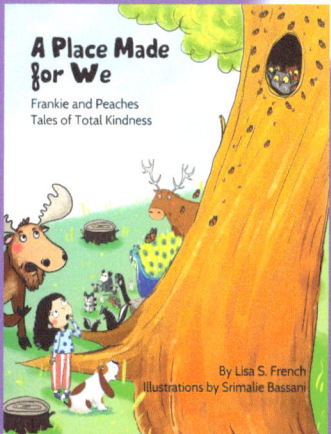

Get your "I Planted a Tree with F&P" poster at
www.favoriteworldpress.com/MakingRoom

CPSIA information can be obtained
at www.ICGtesting.com
Printed in the USA
LVHW070025180619
621463LV00009B/96/P